W9-BYB-142

Juvenile

SCHAUMBURG TOWNSHIP DISTRICT LIBRARY

3 1257 00719 1009

**SCHAUMBURG TOWNSHIP
DISTRICT LIBRARY
130 SOUTH ROSELLE ROAD
SCHAUMBURG, ILLINOIS 60193**

Copyright © 1989 by Nord-Süd Verlag, Mönchaltorf, Switzerland
First published in Switzerland under the title *Mirjams Geschenk*
English translation copyright © 1989 by Rosemary Lanning
North-South Books English language edition copyright © 1989
by Rada Matija AG, 8625 Gossau ZH, Switzerland

All rights reserved. No part of this book may be reproduced or
utilized in any form or by any means, electronic or mechanical,
including photocopying, recording or by any information storage
and retrieval system, without permission in writing from the
Publisher. Printed in Germany. ISBN 1-55858-008-5

1 3 5 7 9 10 8 6 4 2

First published in the United States, Great Britain, Canada,
Australia and New Zealand in 1989 by North-South Books,
an imprint of Rada Matija AG

Library of Congress Catalog Card Number: 89-42611

British Library Cataloguing in Publication Data

Scheidl, Gerda Marie
Miriam's gift.
I. Title II. Pfister, Marcus III. Mirjams
geschenk. *English*
833'.914 [J]

ISBN 1-55858-008-5

Miriam's Gift

A Christmas story by Gerda Marie Scheidl
Translated by Rosemary Lanning
Illustrated by Marcus Pfister

North-South Books
New York

SCHAUMBURG TOWNSHIP DISTRICT LIBRARY
JUVENILE DEPT.
32 WEST LIBRARY LANE
SCHAUMBURG, ILLINOIS 60194

3/90

HOLIDAY
EASY
CHRISTMAS
SCHEIDLIG

3 1257 00719 1009

Elias had pitched his tent close to a cliff, below a range of hills. He had chosen this place with great care so that he and his family would be protected from the wind and frost and wild animals. He had been travelling for a long time, with his wife Sarah, his two sons, their grand-mother and his little daughter, Miriam.

Now they needed to rest. Night had come. Everyone lay down wearily, but rest was not granted to them for long. In the middle of the night shepherds came to their tent, woke them and spoke of angels who had suddenly appeared to them. "They told us of a child who has been born in Bethlehem, in a humble stable. It is the baby Jesus. We are going to welcome him. Will you come?"

Such a journey would be too exhausting for Grandmother, thought Elias. She must stay at home, and Miriam must stay with her.

Outside the wind had become very strong. Elias went to check that the tent ropes were well anchored in the ground. Miriam ran to him and begged, "Please, Father, take me with you. I want to give my doll to the baby Jesus."

Her father smiled, but he said, "You cannot come with us. You are too young. Do you hear the wind? It would blow you and your doll away."

Miriam dared not argue. She went sadly back to her
grandmother who was very wise and would know what
to do.

"Ask the wind to stop blowing," said Grandmother.
Miriam stared at her in disbelief.

"You want me to ask the wind to stop! Will it understand me?"

"Oh yes," said Grandmother. "It will understand
you. And it will reply. Listen carefully."

Grandmother cautiously lifted a corner of the tent and
whispered, "Crawl out this way." Miriam tucked her
doll into her pocket and crept outside.

Whoo-oo-oo . . . The wind almost blew Miriam off her feet. She clung to the cliff with both hands.

"Wind, oh please wind, don't blow so hard," cried Miriam into the powerful gusts. "Or I can't go to Bethlehem. I want to give my doll to the baby Jesus."

Miriam listened. Had the wind heard her at all? She hardly dared breathe.

Then the wind was suddenly still. The gentlest of breezes caressed Miriam's cheek and, as if from afar, she heard a voice: "Go then, little Miriam. Take your doll to the baby Jesus. The air is hardly stirring now."

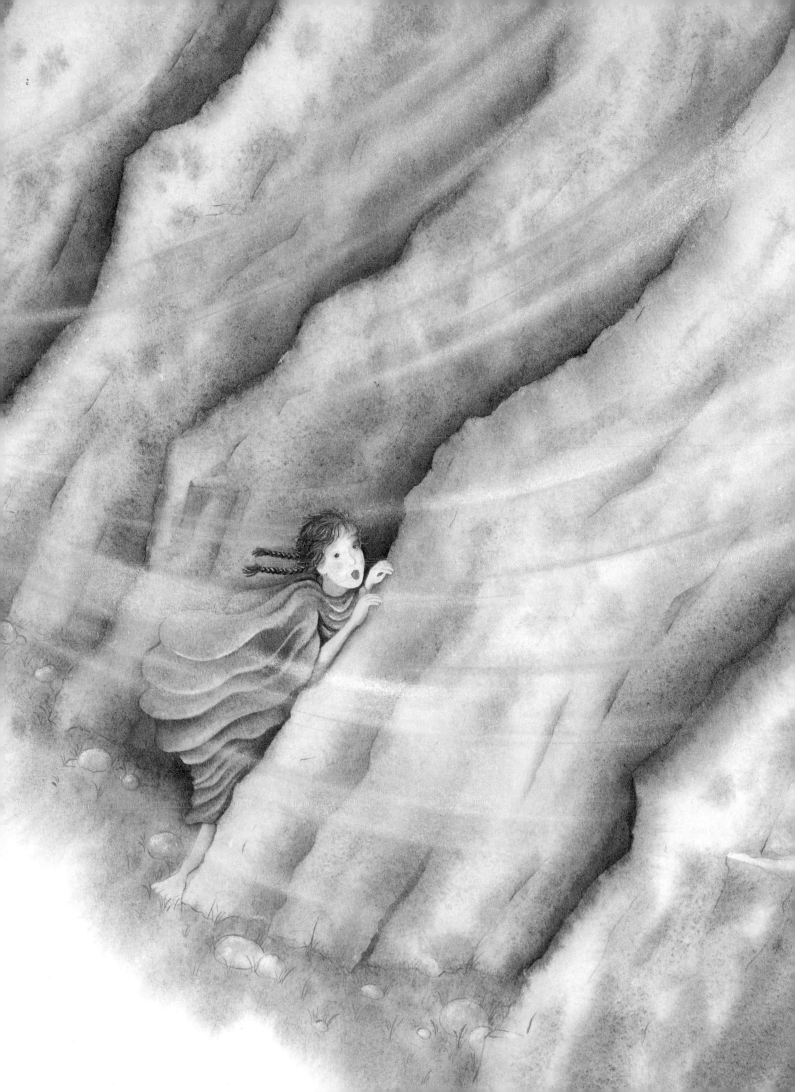

When Miriam crept back into the tent her father stood before her. "Where have you been?" he asked angrily.

"I was outside, talking to the wind." In her excitement, Miriam's words tumbled out. "It promised it would stop blowing. Now I can come to Bethlehem."

"Nonsense! The wind can't talk."

"But Father, can't you feel how still the air has become?"

Elias listened. It was true that the powerful roaring of the wind had ceased.

"No, you may not come," he said. "The frost will freeze your fingers and toes." Miriam said nothing. She ran back to Grandmother.

"Then ask the frost to go away," said Grandmother. "Just outside the tent there is a cavern. The frost lurks in there, breathing its cold breath over the land." Again she lifted a corner of the tent and Miriam crept outside.

Miriam shivered but she went bravely into the cave. It was bitterly cold inside. There was a grinding and tinkling sound from all sides. Miriam was so frightened that she longed to turn back, but she called out courageously, "Frost, oh please frost, stay in your cave, or I won't be allowed to go to Bethlehem and give my doll to the baby Jesus." Miriam listened for any sound from the depths of the cave. The grinding and tinkling had stopped. From far away she heard a voice: "Go then, little Miriam. Give your doll to the baby Jesus. I will withdraw, deep into my cave."

But still her father would not let her go. "The wild animals might harm you," he said sternly. Disappointed, Miriam returned to Grandmother.

Grandmother looked kindly at her. "Ask the Great Bear to command the wild beasts to be tame tonight. Go a little way up the hill and he will come down to you."

Once again Grandmother lifted a corner of the tent and Miriam crept out with her doll.

Far, far above her Miriam saw the Great Bear. She ran up the hill. Something strange was happening. It looked as if the Great Bear was coming closer. She felt frightened, but she cried, "Great Bear, please ask the wild beasts not to be fierce tonight or I won't be allowed to go to Bethlehem to give my doll to the baby Jesus."

The Great Bear lifted his paw and growled, "Go then, little Miriam. I will command the wild beasts to be gentle." Miriam called out, "Thank you!" and ran back into the tent.

She wanted to tell everyone what the Great Bear had promised, but she had no time. Her parents and brothers were ready to leave.

"Be good and helpful to Grandmother," said her father. Then they all set off for Bethlehem.

Miriam sighed as they left her behind. Grand-mother hugged her, dried her tears and said, "You also will go to Bethlehem."

"But how can I find the way on my own, Grand-mother?"

Grandmother stood up and led Miriam outside the tent. She pointed to the sky and said, "Do you see that star that is burning so brightly?" Miriam nodded.

"Follow the star and you will come to Bethlehem."

Miriam held her doll close and started on her way, following the star all the time.

Suddenly a wolf stood in her path. Miriam gasped and stood still.

"Climb onto my back," said the wolf gently, "and I will carry you."

So Miriam climbed trustingly onto the wolf's back.

"Hold on very tight so you won't fall off," said the wolf and he set off with a great bound towards Bethlehem.

The star burned ever more brightly and soon they had reached the stable. "Thank you, kind wolf," whispered Miriam, stroking the animal that had carried her so swiftly through the night. Then she walked towards the stable.

Outside the door stood her father, mother and brothers. Miriam hesitated. But then her father motioned her to come closer, and took her hand.

At last Miriam saw the baby Jesus. She went to the cradle and laid her doll in the straw. The holy child smiled at her. Then Miriam felt full of joy, and so did all those who were with her.

SCHAUMBURG TWP. DISTRICT LIBRARY